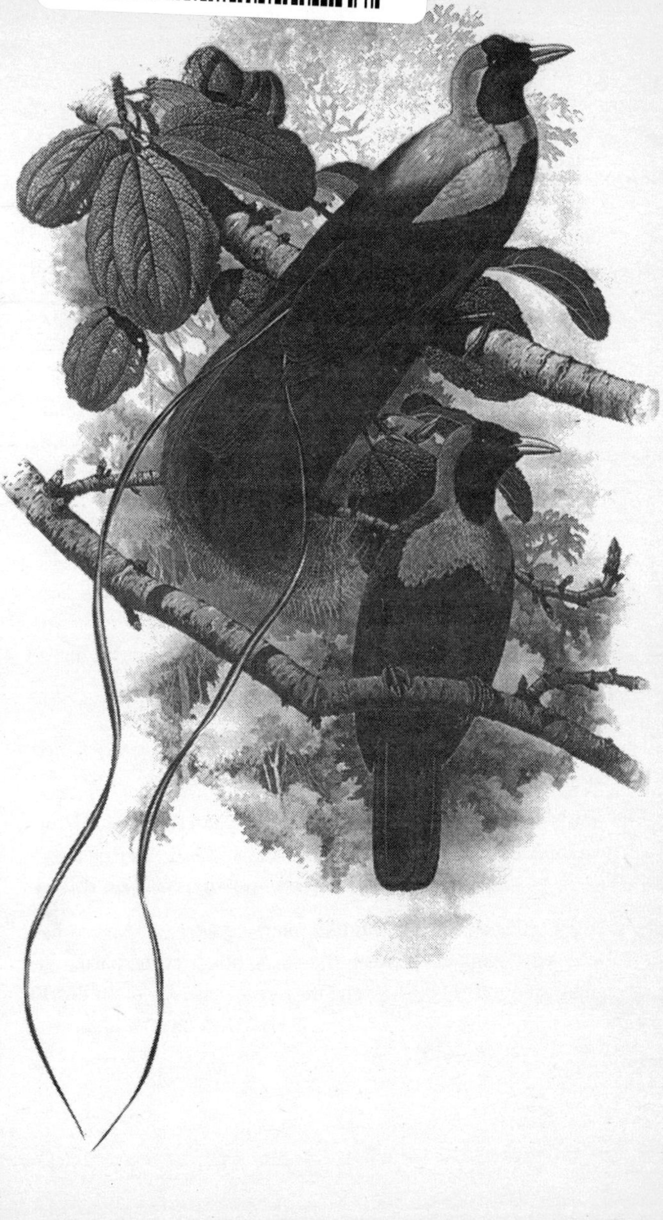

SILK

"*Silk* is a heart-breaking love story, simply told . . . a stylistic tour de force, its rhythms and effects evocative of a crisp and haunting haiku"
GEORDIE GREIG, *Sunday Times*

"This small but perfectly formed novella offers an elegant and unfrenzied entry into [Baricco's] work"
HARRIET PATERSON, *Independent*

"[*Silk*] is the mixture of the fabulous and prosaic found in Márquez and in the best childrens' fiction – *The Little Prince* or Patrick Suskind's *The Story of Mister Summer*. Baricco has created a story of 'Sea-voyages, the smell of mulberries at Lavilledieu, steam trains' but most of all of impossible love, 'Something capable of lifting a life off its hinges.'"
TOBIAS HILL, *The Times*

"Baricco's style is economic to the point of poetry . . . the result is deeply moving"
Guardian

"For all its brevity there is enough in *Silk* to keep the keen deconstructionist busy, but in the final analysis it enchants because it is beautifully, melodically written, deals with love as a higher emotion, and can be read by the fireside in an hour or so . . . A tantalisingly, silken slip of a novel"
JANE CHARTERIS, *Literary Review*

"A remarkable love story that plays on the imagination, and one which has become a bestseller in its native Italy, *Silk* is an enchantment, an exquisite narrative and a stylistic tour de force"
NEIL DODDS, *Northern Woman*

"With stylistic perfection and an intense poetry . . . Baricco has achieved a synthesis between the poetic power of the haiku, the impossible grace of the fuge and the serene sensuality of the novel"
MICHÈLE GAZIER, *Télérama*

ALESSANDRO BARICCO was born in Turin in 1958. He is the author of two previous novels, *Castelli di rabbia*, which won the Prix Médicis and the Campiello prize, and *Oceano mare*, which won the Viareggio and Palazzo del Bosco prizes. He has also written works in the field of musicology. He is highly regarded in Italy for his television programmes, one on opera, the other on literature.

Silk, which became an immediate bestseller in Italy, has been or is to be published in sixteen languages – including Japanese.

GUIDO WALDMAN'S translations from Italian include a prose translation of Ariosto's *Orlando Furioso* and Boccaccio's *Decameron*, both for Oxford University Press World Classics. He was editor of the *Penguin Book of Italian Short Stories*. This translation of *Silk* has been awarded the Weidenfeld Translation Prize.

Alessandro Baricco

SILK

Translated from the Italian
by Guido Waldman

THE HARVILL PRESS
LONDON

First published in Italy with the title *Seta* by Rizzoli, Milan, 1996

This paperback edition first published in Great Britain in 1998 by
The Harvill Press, 2 Aztec Row, Berners Road, London N1 0PW

www.harvill-press.com

7 9 8

A CIP catalogue record for this book is available from the British Library

ISBN 1 86046 366 5

Designed and typeset in Baskerville at Libanus Press, Marlborough

Printed and bound in Great Britain by Mackays of Chatham

Half title illustration by William T. Cooper

SILK

1

Although his father had pictured for him a brilliant future in the army, Hervé Joncour had ended up earning his crust in an unusual career which, by a singular piece of irony, was not unconnected with a charming side that bestowed on it a vaguely *feminine* intonation.

Hervé Joncour bought and sold silkworms for a living.

The year was 1861. Flaubert was writing *Salammbô*, electric light remained hypothetical, and Abraham Lincoln, beyond the Ocean, was fighting a war of which he was not to see the finish.

Hervé Joncour was thirty-two.

He bought and sold.

Silkworms.

———

To be precise, Hervé Joncour bought and sold the silkworms when their being worms consisted in being tiny eggs, yellow or grey in colour, motionless and apparently dead. The palm of one hand could hold thousands of them.

"You could talk of holding a fortune in your hands."

At the beginning of May the eggs hatched, setting free a larva which, after frantically eating its way through mulberry leaves, saw to incarcerating itself afresh in a cocoon, only to escape from it for good two weeks later, leaving behind it a fortune in silk to the tune of a thousand metres of raw thread, and in cash as a handsome sum in French francs: that is assuming that everything went according to plan and, as in the case of Hervé Joncour, you were somewhere in southern France.

Lavilledieu was the name of the town inhabited by Hervé Joncour.

Hélène was that of his wife.

They had no children.

———

In order to avoid the epidemics which were increasingly ravaging the European hatcheries, Hervé Joncour went further afield to acquire the eggs beyond the Mediterranean, in Syria and Egypt. Herein lay the most perfectly adventurous part of his work. He would set out each year early in January. He would travel 1600 miles by sea and 800 miles overland. He would choose the eggs, negotiate the price, make his purchase. Then he would turn round, travel 800 miles overland and 1600 miles by sea and return to Lavilledieu, usually the first Sunday in April, usually in time for High Mass.

He would work for two weeks to prepare the eggs and sell them.

For the rest of the year, he rested.

———

4

"What's Africa like?" they would ask him.

"Tired."

He had a large house just outside the town, and a small laboratory in the centre, directly opposite the deserted house belonging to Jean Berbeck.

Jean Berbeck had decided one day that he was not going to speak ever again. He kept his promise. His wife and two daughters left him. He died. Nobody wanted his house, which is why it was now a deserted house.

Buying and selling silkworms, Hervé Joncour earned each year a sufficient sum to assure himself and his wife of such comforts as pass for luxury in the minds of country dwellers. He enjoyed his possessions discreetly and the prospect, which was not unrealistic, of achieving true wealth left him entirely indifferent. Besides, he was one of those men who like to be *observers* at their own lives, any ambition actually to *participate* in them being considered inappropriate.

It will have been noted that such people observe their destiny much as most people tend to observe a rainy day.

———

Had he been asked, Hervé Joncour would have answered that his life was to continue this way forever after. The epidemic of *pébrine*, however, the spotted disease in silkworm which had made the eggs from European hatcheries unfit for use, spread overseas in the early '60s, as far as Africa and even, some say, as far as India. Hervé Joncour returned from his accustomed voyage in 1861 with a supply of eggs that turned out, two months later, to be almost entirely affected. For Lavilledieu, as for so many other towns whose prosperity was based on silk-production, this year seemed to betoken the beginning of the end. Science appeared incapable of determining the cause of the epidemic. And the whole world even to its outer reaches seemed to have fallen captive to this inexplicable curse.

"*Nearly* the whole world," quietly observed Baldabiou. "Nearly," and he poured two fingers of water into his Pernod.

———

6

Baldabiou was the man who twenty years earlier had come to town, made straight for the mayor's office, stepped in unannounced, laid on his desk a silk scarf the colour of the sunset and asked him:

"D'you know what this is?"

"Woman's stuff."

"Wrong. Man's stuff: money."

The mayor had him thrown out. Baldabiou built a mill down by the river, a shed beside the woods in which to raise the worms, and at the crossroads for Vivier a chapel dedicated to Saint Agnes. He took on some thirty hands, sent to Italy for a mysterious machine made out of wood, all wheels and gears, and did not utter another word for seven months. Then he went back to the mayor and laid on his desk neat piles of large-denomination banknotes to the value of thirty thousand francs.

"D'you know what this is?"

"Money."

"Wrong. It's proof that you're a blockhead."

He gathered them up, dropped them into his bag and made to leave.

The mayor stopped him.

"What the devil am I supposed to do?"

"Nothing: and you'll be mayor of a wealthy town."

Five years later there were seven mills at Lavilledieu, which had become one of Europe's leading centres for the rearing of silkworms and spinning of silk. Baldabiou did not own them all. Other local notables and land-owners had followed him in this curious commercial venture. To each one of them Baldabiou had divulged the secrets of the trade without making difficulties. He derived far greater amusement from this than from making a sackful of money. Teaching. Having secrets to impart. That's the way he was.

———

7

Baldabiou also was the man who eight years previously had changed Hervé Joncour's life. Those were the days when the first epidemics had begun to affect the European output of silkworm eggs. Quite undismayed, Baldabiou had studied the situation and come to the conclusion that the problem was not going to be resolved but had to be circumvented. He had an idea, all he needed was the right man. He realised he had found him when he noticed Hervé Joncour walking past the Café Verdun looking dapper in his infantry subaltern's uniform and proud of his bearing – a soldier on leave. He was twenty-four in those days. Baldabiou invited him home, opened before him an atlas full of exotic names and said to him:

"Congratulations, my boy. At last you've found yourself a serious job."

Hervé Joncour listened to an elaborate tale of silkworms, eggs, Pyramids, sea-voyages. Then he said:

"I can't."

"Why not?"

"My leave's up in two days. I have to return to Paris."

"A military career?"

"Yes. That's what my father's wanted."

"No problem."

He marched Hervé Joncour straight to his father.

"D'you know who this is?" he asked after stepping into the man's study unannounced.

"My son."

"Take another look."

The mayor sagged against the back of his leather armchair and broke into a sweat.

"My son Hervé returns to Paris in two days' time; a brilliant career in our armed forces awaits him there, God and Saint Agnes willing."

"Precisely. Trouble is, God has other fish to fry and Saint Agnes can't stand soldiers."

A month later Hervé Joncour left for Egypt. He travelled on board a ship called *Adel*. Smells from the galley pervaded the cabins, there was an Englishman who said he had fought at Waterloo, on the evening of the third day they saw a flash of dolphin on the horizon like drunken waves, the roulette wheel kept turning up 16.

He was back two months later – the first Sunday in April, in time for High Mass – with thousands of eggs wrapped in cotton wool in two large wooden crates. He had plenty to talk about. But what Baldabiou said to him once they were alone was:

"Tell me about the dolphins."

"The dolphins?"

"About the time when you saw them."

That was Baldabiou for you.

No one knew how old he was.

———

8

"*Nearly* the whole world," quietly observed Baldabiou, pouring two fingers of water into his Pernod.

An August night, past midnight. Normally at that hour the Verdun would have been closed for some while. The chairs were upturned in neat rows on the tables. The counter had been wiped down and everything else. All that remained was to turn out the lights and shut up shop. But Verdun waited: Baldabiou was talking.

Seated facing him, Hervé Joncour listened to him, motionless, a spent cigarette between his lips. As eight years before, he was leaving the man to rewrite his destiny in orderly fashion. His voice came across limpid and quiet, punctuated with periodic sips of Pernod. He did not stop for a minute. The last thing he said was:

"There's no choice. If we want to survive we have to get over there."

Silence.

Verdun, leaning on the counter, lifted his eyes to the pair of them.

Baldabiou concentrated on discovering one further sip of Pernod in the bottom of his glass.

Hervé Joncour laid his cigarette down on the edge of the table before saying:

"This place, Japan, where precisely is it?"

Baldabiou raised the tip of his cane and pointed beyond the roofs of Saint-August.

"That way and keep going."

He said.

"Right to the end of the world."

———

9

In those days Japan was effectively on the other side of the world. It was an island made up of islands, and for two hundred years it had lived entirely cut off from the rest of humanity, refusing all contact with the continent and denying access to all foreigners. The China coast lay some two hundred miles off, but an imperial decree had had the effect of increasing the distance by an island-wide ban on the construction of any vessel carrying more than a single mast. Pursuing a logic that had its own rationale, there was no law against emigration: those who attempted to return, however, were sentenced to death. Chinese, Dutch and English traders had made repeated efforts to breach this absurd isolation, but they had achieved nothing beyond establishing a fragile and risky smugglers' network. All this had yielded them were scanty earnings, much trouble, and the odd legend such as might be retailed in the ports of an evening. But where they had failed the Americans achieved success, thanks to sheer force of arms. In July 1853 Commodore Matthew C. Perry sailed into Yokohama Bay with a modern steam-driven fleet and delivered an ultimatum to the Japanese, which "desired" them to open the island to foreigners.

The Japanese had never before seen a ship that could sail against the wind.

When Perry returned seven months later to receive the reply to his ultimatum, the island's military government conceded its signature to an agreement that would open to foreigners two harbours in the north of the country, and the inauguration of the first measured commercial relations. "The sea around this island," declared the Commodore with a touch of solemnity, "has today become vastly shallower."

———

10

Baldabiou was acquainted with all these stories. Above all he was acquainted with a legend that kept resurfacing in the tales told by those who had been there. It was said that the island produced the finest silk in the world. They had been making silk for a thousand years and more, according to rituals and secrets that had arrived at a state of mystical precision. What went through Baldabiou's mind was that this was no legend but the pure and simple truth. He had once held between his fingers a veil woven out of Japanese silk thread. It was like grasping in your fingers . . . nothing. Thus, when everything seemed to have gone awry on account of the *pébrine* and the diseased eggs, here is what he thought:

"There's an island that's full of silkworms. And an island on which for the last two hundred years not a single Chinese trader or English insurance salesman has succeeded in landing is an island that will never be reached by any disease."

He did not confine himself to thinking this. He said as much to all the silk-manufacturers of Lavilledieu after assembling them at the Café Verdun. Not one of them had ever heard of Japan.

"Are we supposed to cross the world to get there and buy eggs, as God bids us, in a place where they hang foreigners on sight?"

"They used to hang," rectified Baldabiou.

They knew not what to think. Someone thought to object.

"If nobody's thought of going there to buy eggs there has to be a reason."

Baldabiou might have bluffed, considering that what the rest of the world lacked was another Baldabiou. But he preferred to give a straight answer.

"The Japanese have resigned themselves to selling their silk. But not the eggs. They keep a tight grip on those. And should you try to leave the island with any, you're committing a criminal offence."

The silk-manufacturers of Lavilledieu were all gentlemen, more or less, and it would never have crossed their minds to break any law of their country. The notion of doing so on the other side of the world, however, struck them as entirely reasonable.

11

The year was 1861. Flaubert was completing *Salammbô*, electric light remained hypothetical, and Abraham Lincoln, beyond the Ocean, was fighting a war of which he was not to see the finish. The silk-manufacturers of Lavilledieu banded together and put up the considerable sum needed for the expedition, which they all found it logical to entrust to Hervé Joncour. When Baldabiou asked him to accept, he replied with a question.

"This place, Japan, where precisely is it?"

"Just keep going. Right to the end of the world."

He set out on 6 October. On his own.

At the gates of Lavilledieu he hugged his wife Hélène and told her simply:

"You're not to worry about anything."

She was a tall woman, she moved slowly, she had long black hair that she never put up. She had a most beautiful voice.

———

Hervé Joncour set out with eighty thousand francs in gold and the names of three men, supplied to him by Baldabiou: a Chinaman, a Dutchman and a Japanese. He crossed the frontier near Metz, travelled the breadth of Württemberg and Bavaria, entered Austria, reached Vienna and Budapest by train, thence to continue as far as Kiev. He travelled two thousand kilometres of Russian steppe on horseback, crossed the Urals, entered Siberia, continued for forty days until he reached Lake Baikal, known locally as: "the sea". He descended the course of the River Amur, skirting the Chinese border as far as the Ocean, and when he arrived at the Ocean he stopped in the port of Sabirk for eleven days, until a Dutch smugglers' ship conveyed him to Cape Teraya on the west coast of Japan. Taking secondary roads, he crossed the provinces of Ishikawa, Toyama and Niigata on foot, entered the province of Fukushima, and reached the town of Shirakawa, passed to the east of it, waited two days for a man in black who blind-folded him and brought him to a hill village where he spent the night, and the following day he negotiated the purchase of the eggs with a man who did not speak and kept his face covered with a silken veil. Black. At sunset he hid the eggs in his luggage, turned his back on Japan, and set about his return journey.

Barely had he passed the last houses in the village when a man ran up to overtake and stop him. He said something to him in an excited, peremptory tone of voice, then escorted him back, firmly and politely.

Hervé Joncour did not speak Japanese and was unable to understand the man. What he did grasp was that Hara Kei wanted to see him.

———

13

They slid back a rice-paper panel and Hervé Joncour stepped inside. Hara Kei was seated cross-legged on the floor in the furthest corner of the room. He wore a dark tunic and no jewellery. The only visible sign of his authority was a woman lying beside him, motionless, her head in his lap, eyes shut, her arms concealed in the folds of an ample red dress which spread out about her on the ash-coloured mat like flame. He was slowly running a hand through her hair: it was as if he were stroking some luxurious, sleeping animal.

Hervé Joncour crossed the room, awaited a sign from his host, and sat down in front of him. They continued thus in silence, their eyes upon each other. A servant came in unobserved and set two tea cups down in front of them. After which he vanished into thin air. Then Hara Kei began to speak, in his own tongue; he had a singsong voice verging on a sort of falsetto that sounded painfully affected. Hervé Joncour listened. He kept his eyes fixed on those of Hara Kei and only for an instant, as though barely aware of it, did he drop them onto the woman's face.

It was the face of a young girl.

He raised his eyes once more.

Hara Kei broke off, lifted one of the tea cups, carried it to his lips, paused for a moment, then said:

"Try to tell me who you are."

He said this in French, somewhat drawing out the vowels, in a hoarse, sincere voice.

———

To the most elusive man in Japan, master of all that the world contrived to carry off the island, Hervé Joncour attempted to explain who he was. He did so in his own tongue, speaking slowly, not entirely certain whether Hara Kei was able to understand. By instinct he abandoned all caution, and recounted in simple words the entire truth, inventing nothing, omitting nothing. Small details and crucial events he laid out before him in the same flat monotone and with minimal gestures, as though rehearsing the joyless, neutral, hypnotic cadences of one reading a list of objects that have survived a fire. Hara Kei listened, not a flicker of expression disturbing his features. He fixed his gaze on Hervé Joncour's lips as though upon the last lines of a letter of farewell. All was so silent and motionless in the room that what next occurred, though nothing in itself, seemed quite momentous.

Suddenly,

without the smallest movement,

that young girl,

opened her eyes.

Hervé Joncour continued talking but instinctively lowered his eyes to her and what he saw, as he continued talking, was that her eyes *did not have an oriental slant*, and that they were fastened upon him *with a disconcerting intensity*: as though this is what they had been doing from the start, from beneath lowered lids. Hervé Joncour turned his eyes elsewhere, as indifferently as he was able, and tried to pursue his narrative without betraying the smallest alteration in his voice. He broke off only when his eyes lit upon the tea cup placed before him on the floor. He picked it up in one hand, carried it to his lips, drank slowly. Then he resumed his narrative as he set the cup down before him once more.

———

France, sea-voyages, the smell of mulberries at Lavilledieu, steam-trains, Hélène's voice. Hervé Joncour continued the narrative of his life as he had never done in his life before. The girl continued to gaze at him with such a fierce concentration that he felt obliged to charge each word with exceptional meaning. The room seemed to have slipped back into an immutable quiescence when in absolute silence she unexpectedly thrust a hand out from her dress and slid it onto the mat before her. Hervé Joncour noticed this pale blur impinging on the edge of his field of vision; he saw it slide over Hara Kei's tea cup only to continue bizarrely on its path until it unhesitantly grasped the other cup, which could only be the one from which *he* had drunk; her hand picked it up lightly and bore it off. Hara Kei had not for an instant taken his expressionless eyes off Hervé Joncour's lips.

The girl gently raised her head.

For the first time she took her eyes off Hervé Joncour and transferred them to the cup.

Slowly she turned the cup until her lips were at the precise point where he had drunk.

She closed her eyes and took a sip of tea.

She moved the cup from her lips.

She slipped it back to the place from which she had taken it.

She withdrew her hand within her dress.

She rested her head once more in Hara Kei's lap. Her eyes remained open, fixed on those of Hervé Joncour.

Hervé Joncour spoke for a good deal longer. He broke off only when Hara Kei averted his eyes and gave a nod.

Silence.

In French, somewhat drawing out the vowels, in a hoarse, sincere voice Hara Kei said:

"If you wish, I should be glad to see you return."

For the first time he smiled.

"The eggs you have in your possession are fish-eggs, they are worth little more than nothing."

Hervé Joncour lowered his eyes. His tea cup stood there, in front of him. He took it and began to turn it, to scrutinise it as though searching for something along its coloured rim. When he found what he was looking for, he set his lips to it, and drank to the last drop. Then he set the cup down before him and said:

"I know."

Hara Kei chuckled delightedly.

"Is that why you've paid in spurious gold?"

"I've paid for what I've bought."

Hara Kei turned serious again.

"When you leave here you'll have what you want."

"When I leave this island, alive, you'll receive the gold due to you. You have my word."

Hervé Joncour did not even wait for a reply. He stood up, stepped back a few paces, then bowed.

The last thing he saw, before leaving the room, was her eyes, fixed upon him, and perfectly mute.

———

17

Six days later Hervé Joncour boarded a Dutch smugglers' ship at Takaoka, which took him to Sabirk. Thence he skirted the Chinese border as far as Lake Baikal, travelled four thousand kilometres over Siberian soil, crossed the Urals, arrived back in Kiev and crossed the whole of Europe by train, from east to west, until after a three months' voyage he arrived in France. The first Sunday in April – in time for High Mass – he reached the gates of Lavilledieu. He stopped, gave thanks to God, and entered the town on foot, counting his steps, that each one might have a name, and that he might never forget them.

"What's it like, the end of the world?" Baldabiou asked him.

"Invisible."

To his wife Hélène he brought the gift of a silken tunic which she, out of modesty, never wore. If you held it in your hands, it was like grasping nothing.

18

The eggs brought back from Japan by Hervé Joncour, attached to hundreds of slivers of mulberry bark, turned out to be perfectly healthy. Silk production in the region around Lavilledieu was exceptional that year for both quantity and quality. It was decided to open another two silk mills, and Baldabiou built a cloister to the side of Saint Agnes' chapel. The reason is not clear, but he had imagined a circular one and had therefore entrusted the task to a Spanish architect called Juan Benitez, who enjoyed a measure of fame in the department of *Plaza de Toros.*

"No sand, of course, in the middle, but a garden. And if possible dolphins' heads, rather than bulls' heads at the entrance."

"¿Dolphins, *señor*?"

"The fish, Benitez, do you follow me?"

Hervé Joncour went through his accounts a couple of times and discovered himself a wealthy man. He bought thirty acres to the south of his property, and devoted the summer months to designing a park in which it would be balm, perfect quietude, to walk. In his mind it would be invisible, like the end of the world. Every morning he would stroll as far as Verdun's to hear the local gossip and riffle through the newspapers sent down from Paris. In the evenings he would sit endlessly in the porch of his house, next to his wife Hélène. She would read a book, out loud, and this made him happy because he thought there was not in the whole world a voice more beautiful than hers.

He turned thirty-three on 4 September 1862. His life was as rain before his eyes, a vision of peace.

———

"You're not to worry about anything."

As Baldabiou had so decided, Hervé Joncour set out once more for Japan on the first day of October. He crossed the French frontier near Metz, travelled the breadth of Württemberg and Bavaria, entered Austria, reached Vienna and Budapest by train, thence to continue as far as Kiev. He travelled two thousand kilometres of Russian steppe on horseback, crossed the Urals, entered Siberia, continued for forty days until he reached Lake Baikal, known locally as: "the demon". He descended the course of the River Amur, skirting the Chinese border as far as the Ocean, and when he arrived at the Ocean he stopped in the port of Sabirk for eleven days, until a Dutch smugglers' ship conveyed him to Cape Teraya on the west coast of Japan. Taking secondary roads, he crossed the provinces of Ishikawa, Toyama and Niigata on foot, entered the province of Fukushima, and reached the town of Shirakawa, passed to the east of it, waited two days for a man in black who blindfolded him and brought him to the village of Hara Kei. When he was able to reopen his eyes he found himself confronted by two servants who took his luggage and brought him to the edge of a wood where they left him after indicating a path to him. Hervé Joncour set off walking through the shadows made where the trees around and above him cut off the sunlight. He stopped only when suddenly the vegetation opened up for an instant like a window at the edge of the path. A lake came into view, some thirty metres below. By the lakeside Hara Kei was to be seen from behind, squatting down, with a woman in an orange dress, her hair loose on her shoulders. The moment Hervé Joncour saw her she looked slowly round for a second, just long enough to catch his eye.

Her eyes did not have an oriental slant, and her face was the face of a young girl.

Hervé Joncour continued walking in the thick of the wood and emerged to find himself by the edge of the lake. A few paces ahead of him Hara Kei sat on his own, motionless, his back to him, dressed in black. Beside him an orange dress lay abandoned on the ground, and two straw sandals. Hervé Joncour approached. Tiny circular ripples washed the lake-water onto the bank, as though sent hither from a distance.

"My French friend," murmured Hara Kei without looking round.

They spent hours, seated side by side, talking and holding their peace. Then Hara Kei stood up and Hervé Joncour did likewise. Before setting out for the path, with an imperceptible gesture he dropped one of his gloves beside the orange dress lying by the lakeside. It was evening when they reached the village.

33

Hervé Joncour was Hara Kei's guest for four days. It was like living at a king's court. The whole village existed for that man; there was scarcely a single action, up in those hills, that was not to protect him or to do him pleasure. Life was a subdued hum, it proceeded with a studied slackness of pace, like a beast threatened in its lair. The world seemed centuries away.

Hervé Joncour had his own house and five servants who accompanied him wherever he went. He ate alone, in the shade of a tree with coloured blossom he had never seen before. Twice a day he was served tea with a measure of solemnity. In the evening he would be escorted to the largest room in the house; it had a stone floor, and the ritual of the bath was here enacted. Three women of a certain age, their faces coated with a sort of white wax, would pour water over him and dry him with warm silken towels. Their hands were gnarled but their touch as light as could be.

On the morning of the second day Hervé Joncour saw a white man arrive in the village; he was accompanied by two carts crammed with great wooden chests. He was an English-man. He was not there to buy. He was there to sell.

"Arms, *monsieur*. And you?"

"I buy. Silkworms."

They dined together. The Englishman had many stories to tell: he had been travelling back and forth between Europe and Japan for eight years. Hervé Joncour listened to him and only at the end did he ask him:

"Do you know a woman, young, European I believe, white, who lives here?"

The Englishman went on eating, his face impassive.

"White women do not exist in Japan. In Japan there's not a single white woman."

He left the next day, laden with gold.

———

Hervé joncour did not see Hara Kei again until the morning of the third day. He noticed that his five servants had suddenly vanished as if by magic, and a moment later he saw him appear. This man around whom the entire village revolved always moved about inside an empty bubble. As though an unwritten law required him to be left alone.

Together they climbed the hillside until they reached a clearing above which the sky was streaked with the flight of dozens of birds with great blue wings.

"The local people watch their flight and read the future in it."

Said Hara Kei.

"When I was a boy my father took me to a place like this, put his bow into my hands, and told me to shoot at one of them. I did so, and a big bird with blue wings dropped to earth like a stone. 'Read the flight of your arrow,' my father told me, 'if you want to know your future.'"

They flew slowly, rising and falling in the sky, as if they wanted scrupulously to erase it with their wings.

They returned to the village, walking in the strange afternoon light that had the appearance of evening. On reaching Hervé Joncour's house they bade each other farewell. Hara Kei turned and set off at a leisurely pace, down the road that ran by the riverside. Hervé

Joncour remained standing on his threshold, watching him: he waited till the other was some twenty paces off, then said:

"When will you tell me about that young girl?"

Hara Kei continued walking at a leisurely pace that betokened not a trace of weariness. There reigned all about the most absolute silence, emptiness. As though some singular law dictated that, wherever he went, that man was to go in a complete, unqualified solitude.

———

22

On the morning of the last day, Hervé Joncour left the house and went wandering about the village. He came upon men who bowed as he passed, and women who lowered their eyes and smiled at him. He knew he was close to Hara Kei's house when he saw a huge aviary containing an incredible number of birds, of every species: a spectacle. Hara Kei had told him how he had had them brought to him from every corner of the world. There were some whose value exceeded that of all the silk Lavilledieu could produce in a year. Hervé Joncour stopped to look at this magnificent extravagance. He remembered having read in a book that in the East men wishing to honour the fidelity of their mistresses did not customarily give them jewellery; they gave them the most beautiful, rare birds.

Hara Kei's house seemed to be flooded in a lake of silence. Hervé Joncour drew close and stopped a few yards from the entrance. There were no doors, and on the paper walls there was a play of shadows that appeared and disappeared leaving not a trace of noise. It had no resemblance to life; if there were a name for all this, it was: theatre. Hervé Joncour stopped to wait, not knowing what for; he stood stock-still, a few yards from the house. For the entire interval he conceded to fate, shadows and silences were all that this bizarre stage would vouchsafe.

Therefore Hervé Joncour eventually turned and resumed his walk home at a brisk pace. He bent his head and watched his steps, for this helped him to avoid thinking.

———

That evening Hervé Joncour packed his bags. Then he let himself be brought into the big stone-floored room for the ritual of the bath. He lay down, closed his eyes, and thought about the big aviary, that crazy love-token. A damp cloth was placed over his eyes. This they had never done before. Instinctively he made to remove it, but a hand took hold of his and stopped him. It was not the old hand of an old woman.

Hervé Joncour felt the water run down his body, first on his legs, then down his arms, and on his chest. Water like oil. And all around, a strange silence. He felt the lightness of a silken veil dropping onto him. And the hands of a woman – of a woman – drying him all over, caressing his skin: those hands and that material spun out of nothing. He never stirred, not even when he felt the hands move from his shoulders to his neck and the fingers – the silk and the fingers – climb to his lips and brush them once, slowly, then vanish.

Hervé Joncour then felt the silken veil stand up and move away from him. The last thing was a hand that opened his and placed something in his palm.

He waited a long while, in silence, without moving. Then slowly he removed the damp cloth from his eyes. In the room there remained barely any light. Around him there was nobody. He stood up, took the tunic which lay folded on the floor, draped it round his shoulders, left the room, crossed the house until he stood by his mat, and lay down. He set himself to watching the tiny flame that fluttered in the lamp. And carefully he brought Time to a halt, for as long as he wished.

It was nothing to open his palm, then, and see that scrap of paper. Tiny. A few ideograms drawn one beneath the other. Black ink.

———

The next day, early in the morning Hervé Joncour left. Concealed in his luggage he carried thousands of silkworm eggs, and in other words Lavilledieu's future, and employment for hundreds of people, and wealth for a dozen of them. Where the road curved to the left, hiding the view of the village for good behind the shoulder of the hill, he stopped, giving no thought to the two men escorting him. He dismounted and tarried a little at the side of the road, his eyes fixed on those houses climbing up the hillside.

Six days later Hervé Joncour boarded a Dutch smugglers' ship at Takaoka, which took him to Sabirk. Thence he skirted the Chinese border as far as Lake Baikal, travelled four thousand kilometres over Siberian soil, crossed the Urals, arrived back in Kiev and crossed the whole of Europe by train, from east to west, until after a three months' voyage he arrived in France. The first Sunday in April – in time for High Mass – he reached the gates of Lavilledieu. He saw his wife Hélène run up to him, he smelled the perfume of her skin when he embraced her, and heard the velvet in her voice when she said to him:

"You're back."

Softly.

"You're back."

At Lavilledieu life continued simply, governed by order and method. For forty-one days Hervé Joncour let it wash over him. On the forty-second day he surrendered, drew open a drawer inside his cabin-trunk, pulled out a map of Japan, opened it and extracted the slip of paper he had concealed inside it, months earlier. A handful of ideograms drawn one beneath the other. Black ink. He sat down at his desk and gazed at it for a long time.

He found Baldabiou at Verdun's, at the billiard table. He always played alone, against himself. Odd games. The fit against the handicapped is what he called them. He would make a normal stroke, and the next one he would make using only one hand. "The day the handicapped one wins," he would say, "I'll leave this town." The handicapped one had been losing for years.

"Baldabiou, I have to find someone here who can read Japanese."

The handicapped player hit a cannon off two cushions and re-spotted the ball.

"Ask Hervé Joncour, he knows everything."

"I can't make out a word of it."

"You're the Japanese round here."

"I still can't make out a word of it."

The fit player bent over the cue and hit a cannon for six points.

"That only leaves Madame Blanche. She keeps a draper's shop at Nîmes. Above the shop there's a brothel. She owns that too. She's rich. And she's Japanese."

"Japanese? How did she fetch up here?"

"Don't ask her, if you want any favour from her. Damn!"

The handicapped player had just missed a three-cushion cannon worth fourteen points.

Hervé Joncour told his wife Hélène he had to go to Nîmes, on business. And that he would be back the same day.

He climbed to the first floor, above the draper's, at 12 rue Moscat, and asked for Madame Blanche. They kept him waiting a long time. The room was got up as though for a party that had started years ago and never ended. The girls were all young and French. There was a pianist playing tunes that sounded Russian; he used the soft pedal. At the end of each piece he would run his right hand through his hair and murmur:

"*Voilà*."

———

Hervé Joncour waited a couple of hours. Then they took him along a corridor to the door at the end. He opened it and went in.

Madame Blanche was seated in a large armchair by the window. She wore a lightweight kimono: completely white. On her fingers, as though they were rings, she wore little flowers of a deep blue. Shiny black hair, oriental features, perfection.

"What makes you think you're so rich you can come to bed with me?"

Hervé Joncour remained standing in front of her, hat in hand.

"I need a favour from you. Never mind the price."

Then he took from the inside pocket of his jacket a little slip folded in four, and handed it to her.

"I have to know what is written on it."

Madame Blanche did not move a muscle. Her lips were slightly parted – the dawn of a smile.

"Please, *madame.*"

There was no reason on earth why she should do it. Still, she took the slip, opened it, looked at it. She raised her eyes to Hervé Joncour, lowered them again. Slowly she refolded the slip. As she leaned forward to hand it back, her kimono fell open fractionally on her breast. Hervé Joncour noticed that she wore nothing underneath, and that her skin was youthful, white.

"Come back, or I shall die."

She said this in a cold voice, looking Hervé Joncour in the eye, and without betraying the slightest expression.

Come back, or I shall die.

Hervé Joncour returned the slip to the inside pocket of his jacket.

"Thank you."

He gave a nod, turned, made for the door, and was about to place a few banknotes on the table.

"Forget about it."

Hervé Joncour hesitated a moment.

"I'm not speaking of the money. I'm speaking of the woman. Forget about her. She won't die and you know it."

Without turning, Hervé Joncour set the notes down on the table, opened the door and left.

———

Baldabiou said that sometimes people came from Paris to make love to Madame Blanche. On returning to the capital they would wear in the button-hole of their evening dress one or two little blue flowers, the ones she always wore on her fingers like so many rings.

———

29

That summer, for the first time in his life, Hervé Joncour took his wife to the Riviera. They put up for two weeks at a hotel in Nice frequented by Englishmen for the most part and noted for the musical evenings it offered its clientele. Hélène had persuaded herself that in such a lovely spot they would succeed in conceiving the child they had awaited for years in vain. They both decided it would be a boy. And that he would be called Philippe. They took modest advantage of the social round in this resort, only to enjoy themselves, once alone in their room, making fun of the odd characters they had met. One evening at a concert they met a fur-trader, a Pole; he said he had been in Japan.

The night before leaving, Hervé Joncour happened to wake while it was still dark, and get up and approach Hélène's bed. When she opened her eyes he heard his own voice murmuring:

"I shall always love you."

———

At the beginning of September the Lavilledieu silk manufacturers held a meeting to decide a plan of action. The government had sent to Nîmes a young biologist who was to make a study of the disease that was effectively making French silkworm eggs unusable. His name was Louis Pasteur. He worked with microscopes that made it possible to see what was invisible. It was said that he had already achieved extraordinary results. News came from Japan to the effect that a civil war was about to erupt, fomented by the forces in opposition to the opening of the country to foreigners. The French consulate, recently established in Yokohama, sent despatches that discouraged commercial ties with the island for the present; it was suggested that more propitious times should be awaited. Inclined as they were towards caution, and awake to the huge cost entailed by each of these clandestine expeditions to Japan, many of the Lavilledieu notables argued in favour of suspending Hervé Joncour's voyages, and relying for this year on the more or less trustworthy consignments of eggs imported from the Middle East by the big dealers. Baldabiou listened to what they all had to say without uttering a word. When it was finally his turn to speak, what he did was to lay his stick on the table and look at the man sitting opposite him. And wait.

Hervé Joncour knew about Pasteur's research, and had read the despatches from Japan; but he had always refused to comment on them. He preferred to devote his time to titivating his plan for the park he wanted to lay out round his house. In a hidden corner of his study he kept a scrap of paper folded in four, with its handful of ideograms drawn one beneath the other, in black ink. He possessed a substantial bank account, led a quiet life, and nurtured the not unreasonable illusion of imminent fatherhood. When Baldabiou looked up at him what Hervé Joncour said was:

"You decide, Baldabiou."

———

Hervé Joncour left for Japan at the beginning of October. He crossed the French frontier near Metz, travelled the breadth of Württemberg and Bavaria, entered Austria, reached Vienna and Budapest by train, thence to continue as far as Kiev. He travelled two thousand kilometres of Russian steppe on horseback, crossed the Urals, entered Siberia, continued for forty days until he reached Lake Baikal, known locally as: "the last". He descended the course of the River Amur, skirting the Chinese border as far as the Ocean, and when he arrived at the Ocean he stopped in the port of Sabirk for ten days, until a Dutch smugglers' ship conveyed him to Cape Teraya on the west coast of Japan. What he found there was a country in disarray, expecting a war that was unable to erupt. He travelled for days with no need for recourse to his normal measures of prudence, for the map of the distribution of power round about him and the network of controls appeared to have dissolved in the expectation of an explosion that would have left them all completely redrawn. At Shirakawa he met the man who was to bring him to Hara Kei. Two days on horseback brought them within sight of the village. Hervé Joncour entered on foot so that news of his arrival might precede him.

32

They brought him to one of the last houses in the village, high up, backing onto the woods. Five servants awaited him. He entrusted his luggage to them and went out onto the verandah. He could make out Hara Kei's palace on the far side of the village, barely larger than the other houses, but surrounded by huge cedars that protected its solitude. Hervé Joncour continued to look at it, as though there stood nothing else between here and the horizon. Thus he saw,

finally,

suddenly,

the sky above the palace spotted with thousands of birds in flight, as though they had exploded from the earth, birds of every kind, flying all over the place in frantic terror, singing and crying, an explosive fireworks of wings, clouds of colour shot against the light, sounds of terror, music in flight, fleeing through the sky.

Hervé Joncour smiled.

———

33

The village began to swarm like an ant hill run amok; everybody was running about and screaming and watching the flight of the birds that had escaped; for years they had been the pride of their owner, now they were a mockery on wings in the sky. Hervé Joncour left his house and strolled back down through the village, looking ahead of him as calmly as could be. Nobody seemed to notice him and he seemed oblivious of everything. He was a thread of gold running straight through the pattern of a carpet woven by a madman. He crossed the bridge over the river, descended as far as the great cedars, entered their shade and re-emerged. Before him he saw the huge aviary completely empty, its doors gaping wide. In front of it he saw a woman. Hervé Joncour did not look around him but simply continued his slow walk and stopped only when he stood before her.

Her eyes did not have an oriental slant, and her face was the face of a young girl.

Hervé Joncour took a step towards her, reached out his hand and opened it. In his palm he held a scrap of paper, folded in four. She saw it and a smile lit up her entire face. She rested her hand on Hervé Joncour's, clasped it gently, paused a moment, then withdrew it clutching between her fingers this scrap of paper that had been round the world. Barely had she concealed it in a fold of her dress when Hara Kei's voice was to be heard:

54

"Welcome, my French friend."

He stood but a few paces off. Dark kimono, black hair perfectly gathered at the nape of the neck. He approached. He scrutinised the aviary, looking at the open doors one by one.

"They'll be back. It is always hard to resist the temptation to return, don't you find?"

Hervé Joncour did not reply. Hara Kei looked him in the eye and gently told him:

"Come with me."

Hervé Joncour followed him. He took a few steps then turned to the girl and sketched a bow.

"I hope to see you again soon."

Hara Kei continued walking.

"She does not know your language."

He spoke:

"Come."

———

That evening Hara Kei invited Hervé Joncour to his house. There were a few men from the village, and women dressed in the height of elegance, their faces painted white and in gaudy colours. Sake was being drunk, and long wooden pipes were being smoked, an acrid, stupefying tobacco. Tumblers made their appearance, and a man who provoked laughter with his imitations of humans and animals. Three old women played stringed instruments, with fixed smiles on their faces. Hara Kei sat in the place of honour, dressed in dark clothing, bare-footed. Beside him sat the woman with the face of a young girl, dressed in a resplendent silk robe. Hervé Joncour was at the far end of the room: he was besieged by the sickly-sweet perfume of the women surrounding him, and smiled at the men who were happily sharing anecdotes with him, embarrassed though he was that he could not understand them. Time and again he sought her eyes, and she sought and found his. It was a sort of unhappy dance, secret and unfulfilling. Hervé Joncour danced it until late into the night, then he stood up, made his excuses in French, somehow contrived to fend off a woman who was determined to escort him; he elbowed his way through clouds of smoke and men addressing him in their incomprehensible tongue, and left. Before leaving the room he cast one final glance in her direction. She was gazing at him out of the most silent of eyes, for endless ages.

Hervé Joncour wandered round the village, breathing the fresh night air and losing himself up the pathways that climbed the hillside. On reaching his house he noticed a lighted lantern swaying back and forth behind the paper walls. He went in and found two women standing before him. A young oriental girl in a simple white kimono. And her. Her eyes radiated a sort of feverish gaiety. She gave him no time to react. She approached him, took one of his hands, carried it to her face, brushed it with her lips, then, grasping it tightly, placed it on the hands of the girl next to her, and held it there for a moment so that it could not escape. Eventually she withdrew her hand, stepped back two paces, took up the lantern, fixed her eyes for an instant on those of Hervé Joncour, then hastened off. The lantern was orange. She vanished into the night, a little light fleeing away.

———

Hervé Joncour had never seen that girl, nor in truth did he really see her that night. In the unlit room he felt the beauty of her body and recognised her hands and her mouth. He made love to her for hours, using gestures he had never made before, and let himself be taught an unhurried pace hitherto unknown to him. In the dark it took nothing to make love to this girl and not to *her*.

A little before daybreak the girl got up, put on her white kimono and left.

———

In the morning Hervé Joncour found one of Hara Kei's men waiting for him in front of the house. He had fifteen strips of mulberry bark completely covered with eggs: tiny, ivory-coloured. Hervé Joncour carefully inspected each strip of bark, then negotiated the price and paid in gold chips. Before the man left Hervé Joncour conveyed to him that he wished to see Hara Kei. The man shook his head. Hervé Joncour understood from the man's gestures that Hara Kei had left early that morning with his retinue, and nobody knew when he would be back.

Hervé Joncour ran the length of the village to Hara Kei's house. All he found there were servants who answered his every question with a shake of the head. The house looked deserted. And however hard he searched about him, fixing on the most trifling objects, he saw nothing that looked like a message for him. He left the house and on his way back to the village passed the huge aviary. The doors were once more closed. Inside, hundreds of birds were flitting about, sheltered from the sky.

———

Hervé Joncour waited a further two days for a signal of some sort, then set out.

Not half an hour from the village he came upon a strange, silvery sound. Hidden among the leaves there could be made out thousands of dark spots occasioned by a flock of birds at rest. Giving no explanation to the two men escorting him, Hervé Joncour drew rein, unholstered his revolver and fired six shots into the air. The startled flock of birds rose into the air like a cloud of smoke released from a house on fire. The flock was so vast it could have been spotted at a distance of several days' march from there. It darkened the sky, with no goal other than its own fright.

38

Six days later Hervé Joncour boarded a Dutch smugglers' ship at Takaoka, which took him to Sabirk. Thence he skirted the Chinese border as far as Lake Baikal, travelled four thousand kilometres over Siberian soil, crossed the Urals, arrived back in Kiev and crossed the whole of Europe by train, from east to west, until after a three months' voyage he arrived in France. The first Sunday in April – in time for High Mass – he reached the gates of Lavilledieu. He stopped the carriage and for a few minutes remained seated, motionless, behind the drawn curtains. Then he alighted and continued on foot, step after step, with infinite weariness.

Baldabiou asked him if he had seen the war.

"Not the one I was expecting," he replied.

That night he got into Hélène's bed and made love to her so impatiently that she took fright and could not repress her tears. When he noticed this she tried to force a smile for him.

"It's only that I'm so happy," she told him softly.

———

Hervé Joncour consigned the eggs to the Lavilledieu silkbreeders. Then for days he did not appear in the town, even neglecting his daily visit to Verdun's, hitherto a settled habit. Early in May he excited general astonishment by acquiring the house abandoned by Jean Berbeck, the man who had given up speaking from one day to the next and had not uttered another word until his dying day. Everyone thought his idea was to turn it into his new laboratory. He did not even make a start on clearing it out. He would go there from time to time and would tarry alone in those rooms, nobody knew to what purpose.

One day he brought Baldabiou with him.

"Do you know why Jean Berbeck stopped talking?" he asked him.

"That's one of the many things he never said."

Years had passed, but the pictures were still up on the walls, the saucepans on the draining-board beside the sink. Not a happy sight, and Baldabiou, for his part, would have been glad to leave. But Hervé Joncour continued to stare in fascination at those lifeless, mildewed walls. It was obvious: there was something there he was looking for.

"Perhaps sometimes life shows you a side of itself which leaves you with nothing more to say."

He said.

"Nothing more, never."

Baldabiou was not really cut out for serious discussions. He gaped at Jean Berbeck's bed.

"Perhaps anybody would have lost their speech, in such a grim house."

For days Hervé Joncour pursued his life in retreat, scarcely appearing in town, and devoting his time to working on his plans for the park he would lay out sooner or later. He would cover sheet after sheet with strange sketches looking like machines. One evening Hélène asked him:

"What are they?"

"It's an aviary."

"An aviary?"

"Yes."

"What for?"

Hervé Joncour kept his eyes on the sketches.

"You fill it up with birds, as many as you can, then one day when something good happens to you, you throw it open and watch them fly away."

40

At the end of June Hervé Joncour left with his wife for Nice. They took a small villa by the seashore. This had been Hélène's wish, convinced as she was that the tranquillity of an out-of-the-way retreat might succeed in alleviating the depression that seemed to have taken hold of her husband. She had nonetheless been shrewd enough to make it pass for a whim of his own, thus according to the man she loved the satisfaction of seeing his whim humoured.

They enjoyed three weeks of modest, unassailable contentment. On the days when the heat was sufficiently moderate they would hire a trap and take pleasure in discovering the villages hidden up in the hills, from where the sea looked like a backdrop of coloured paper. Occasionally they would venture into town for a concert or social event. One evening they accepted an invitation from an Italian baron who was celebrating his sixtieth birthday with a formal dinner at the Hôtel Suisse. They had reached the dessert when Hervé Joncour happened to look across to Hélène. She was seated on the other side of the table, next to a charming English gentleman who, curiously, sported in the buttonhole of his tail-coat a little garland of tiny blue flowers. Hervé Joncour observed him lean towards Hélène and whisper something in her ear. Hélène burst out laughing, the prettiest of laughs, and as she did so she leaned slightly towards the English gentleman, brushing his shoulder with her hair, in a gesture entirely devoid of embarrassment, but suggesting rather a disconcerting meticulousness. Hervé Joncour looked down at his plate. He could not but notice that his hand, which tightly grasped a silver dessert spoon, was indubitably shaking.

Later in the smoking-room Hervé Joncour, staggering on account of the excessive alcohol he had drunk, approached a man who was sitting alone at the table staring in front of him with a rather absent look on his face. He leant towards him and slowly remarked:

"I have something most important to tell you, *monsieur*. We're all disgusting. We're all marvellous, and we're all disgusting."

The man was from Dresden. He dealt in calves and understood little French. He burst into uproarious laughter, nodding repeatedly: it looked as if he would never stop.

Hervé Joncour and his wife continued their stay on the Riviera into the beginning of September. They left the little villa with regret because amid those walls their call to love each other had lain lightly upon them.

———

Baldabiou arrived at Hervé Joncour's house first thing in the morning. They sat down in the porch.

"Not much of a park, is it?"

"I've not yet started making it, Baldabiou."

"Oh."

Baldabiou never smoked in the morning. He pulled out his pipe, filled and lit it.

"I've met that fellow Pasteur. He knows what's what. He's shown me. He's able to tell the infested eggs from the sound ones. He can't cure them, of course. But he can pick out the sound ones. And he says that probably thirty per cent of the ones we produce are sound."

Pause.

"They say that war has broken out in Japan, I mean properly this time. The English are arming the government, and the Dutch the insurgents. They seem agreed on that. They give them plenty of rope, then they grab everything and share it out between them. The French consulate observes it all, all those people do is look on. They're only fit for sending despatches about massacres and foreigners with their throats slit like sheep."

Pause.

"Any coffee left?"

Hervé Joncour poured him some coffee.

Pause.

"Those two Italians, Ferreri and the other, the ones who went to China last year . . . they came back with eggs, good stock, fifteen thousand ounces; Bollet's people also bought some, they say the stuff was first-class. They're off again in a month . . . they're proposing a good deal, their prices are reasonable, eleven francs the ounce, the whole lot insured. They're dependable, they have a solid organisation behind them, they're selling eggs to half of Europe. Reliable folk, I'm telling you."

Pause.

"I don't know. Maybe we could manage. With our eggs, and Pasteur's work, plus whatever we can buy from the two Italians . . . we might get by. In town the others are saying it's madness sending you over there again . . . with all the expense involved . . . they say it's too risky, and they're right there, the other times it was different, but now . . . now it's not easy to get back alive."

Pause.

"The fact is, they don't want to lose the eggs. And I don't want to lose you."

Hervé Joncour gazed out for a while over the park that did not exist. Then he did a thing he had never done before.

"I'm going to Japan, Baldabiou."

He said.

"I'm going to buy those eggs, with my own money if I have to. All you have to decide is whether I'm selling them to you or to someone else."

Baldabiou was not expecting that. It was like seeing the handicapped one winning, at the final stroke, off four cushions, an impossible geometry.

42

Baldabiou made it known to the Lavilledieu silk-breeders that Pasteur was unreliable, that the two Italians had already swindled half of Europe, that the war in Japan would be over before winter, and that in a dream Saint Agnes had asked him if the lot of them were not a bunch of ninnies. Hélène was the only person to whom he could not lie.

"Does he really have to go, Baldabiou?"

"No."

"Then why?"

"I can't stop him. If he insists on going there, all I can do is give him another reason for coming back."

All the Lavilledieu silk-manufacturers contributed their share to the financing of the expedition, however reluctantly. Hervé Joncour started his preparations and early in October was ready to set out. As every year, Hélène helped him, with no questions asked, and keeping any anxieties to herself. Only on the last evening, after putting out the lamp, did she find the strength to say to him:

"Promise you'll come back."

In a firm voice, austerely.

"Promise you'll come back."

In the dark Hervé Joncour replied:

"I promise."

43

On 10 October 1864 Hervé Joncour left on his fourth journey to Japan. He crossed the French frontier near Metz, travelled the breadth of Württemberg and Bavaria, entered Austria, reached Vienna and Budapest by train, thence to continue as far as Kiev. He travelled two thousand kilometres of Russian steppe on horseback, crossed the Urals, entered Siberia, continued for forty days until he reached Lake Baikal, known locally as: "the holy". He descended the course of the River Amur, skirting the Chinese border as far as the Ocean, and when he arrived at the Ocean he stopped in the port of Sabirk for eight days, until a Dutch smugglers' ship conveyed him to Cape Teraya on the west coast of Japan. Taking secondary roads, he crossed the provinces of Ishikawa, Toyama and Niigata on horseback, and entered the province of Fukushima. When he reached Shirakawa he found the city half destroyed and a garrison of government troops camped amid the ruins. He skirted to the east of the city and awaited Hara Kei's emissary for five days in vain. At dawn on the sixth day he left for the hills to the north. He had few and sketchy maps and what little he could remember. He wandered for days until he recognised a river, then a wood, then a road. At the end of the road he found Hara Kei's village: completely burnt down: houses, trees, everything.

There was nothing left.

There was not a living soul.

Hervé Joncour stood motionless, gazing at that enormous spent brazier. Behind him lay a road eight thousand kilometres long. In front of him, nothing. He had a sudden glimpse of what he had considered invisible.

The end of the world.

———

44

Hervé Joncour spent three hours amid the ruins of the village. He could not bring himself to leave even though he knew that every hour wasted there could spell disaster for him and for the whole of Lavilledieu: he had no silkworm eggs, and even had he been able to find some, he had only a couple of months left to recross the world before they hatched en route, turning into a mass of useless grubs. Even a single day's delay could mean the end. He recognised this, and yet he could not tear himself away. So he remained there until a surprising thing occurred, without rhyme or reason: all of a sudden a little boy stepped out of nowhere. He was dressed in rags and ambled along, eyeing the stranger apprehensively. Hervé Joncour did not move. The little boy took a few more steps then stopped. They stood looking at each other, a few paces apart. Then the child took something out of his rags and, shaking with fear, approached Hervé Joncour and handed it to him. A glove. Hervé Joncour saw in his mind's eye a lake, and an orange dress lying on the ground, and the ripples washing against the bank as though sent thither from a distance. He took the glove and smiled at the boy.

"It's me, the Frenchman . . . the silk person, the Frenchman, understand? . . . It's me."

The boy stopped trembling.

"Frenchman . . . "

The boy's eyes were tear-bright, but he laughed.

He began to speak in a rush, he was almost shouting, and he ran off, signalling Hervé Joncour to follow him. He disappeared up a path that entered the wood, leading towards the mountains.

Hervé Joncour did not move. He turned the glove about in his hands, as though it were all that was left of a vanished world. He knew it was now too late. And that he had no choice.

He stood up. Slowly he returned to his horse. He mounted. Then he did an odd thing. He dug his heels into the animal's flanks. And left. Towards the wood, following the little boy, to beyond the end of the world.

———

They travelled north for days, through the mountains. Hervé Joncour did not know where they were going; he let the little boy be his guide, without trying to ask him anything. They came to two villages. The inhabitants were all hiding indoors. The women fled. The boy had a great lark shouting incomprehensible remarks at their backs. He was no more than fourteen years old. He was forever blowing into a little reed pipe, drawing out of it the calls of every bird in the world. He looked like a person engaged in the happiest act of his life.

On the fifth day they arrived at the top of a hill. The boy indicated a point ahead of them, on the road leading down into the valley. Hervé Joncour took out his spyglass and what he saw was a sort of procession: armed men, women and children, carts, livestock. An entire village: on the move. Mounted and dressed in black was, Hervé Joncour saw, Hara Kei. Behind him a litter came swaying along, its four sides curtained off in gaudy drapes.

———

46

The boy slid off the horse, made some observation and hastened away. Before he disappeared into the trees he turned back and paused for an instant, in search of some gesture to convey that it had been a most lovely journey.

"It's been a most lovely journey," Hervé Joncour called out to him. All that day Hervé Joncour followed the caravan at a distance. When he saw it stop for the night, he continued along the road until he was approached by three armed men, who took charge of his horse and his baggage and led him to a tent. He waited a long time, then Hara Kei appeared. He offered him no greeting. He did not even sit down.

"How have you arrived here, Frenchman?"

Hervé Joncour made no reply.

"I have asked who it was who brought you here."

Silence.

"Here there is nothing for you. There is only war. And it's not your war. Be gone."

Hervé Joncour pulled out a small leather purse, opened it and tipped its contents onto the ground. Gold chips.

"War is a costly game. You have need of me. And I of you."

Hara Kei did not spare a glance for the gold scattered on the ground. He turned on his heel and left.

Hervé Joncour spent the night on the edge of the camp. Nobody spoke to him, nobody seemed to see him. Everyone slept on the ground, by the fires. There were only two tents. Next to one of them Hervé Joncour saw the litter, empty; hanging at its four corners were small cages – birds. Tiny golden bells dangled from the netting of the cages. They jingled lightly in the night-time breeze.

———

48

On awakening he saw the village preparing to resume its journey. The tents were gone. The litter was still there; it stood open. People were boarding the carts in silence. He stood up and took a careful look round; the eyes that caught his were only ones with an oriental slant, and these would be instantly lowered. He saw armed men and children who were not crying. He saw the stony faces that people have when they are in flight. And he saw a tree by the side of the road. Hanging from a branch, by the neck, was the little boy who had led him this far.

Hervé Joncour approached and stood for a while watching him as though in a trance. Then he untied the rope secured to the tree, gathered up the body of the little boy, laid it on the ground and knelt beside it. He could not tear his eyes away from that face. So he did not see the village setting out; he only heard what seemed the far-off sound of the caravan as it brushed past him on its way up the road. He did not look up, not even when he heard the voice of Hara Kei, just a step away, observing to him:

"Japan is an ancient country, you understand? It has ancient laws: the law says there are twelve crimes for which it is licit to condemn a man to death. And one of them is when a servant carries a billet-doux from his mistress."

Hervé Joncour did not take his eyes off the boy who had been killed.

"He had no billet-doux on his person."

"He *was* a billet-doux."

Hervé Joncour felt something press down on his head and force it towards the ground.

"This is a rifle, Frenchman. Keep your eyes down, please."

Hervé Joncour did not understand at first. Then his ears picked up, as the fleeing caravan shuffled past him, the golden sound of a thousand tiny bells approaching little by little, climbing towards him along the road, step after step, and although nothing presented itself to his gaze but that dark earth, he could see the litter in his mind's eye, as it swayed like a pendulum, he as good as saw it coming up the road, yard after yard, and approaching slowly but surely, borne along on that sound which grew ever louder, unbearably loud, ever closer, close enough to brush past him, a gilded sound, right there beside him now, precisely next to him, at that moment – that woman, beside him.

Hervé Joncour raised his head.

Superb materials, silk, the litter was enveloped in it, in a thousand hues, orange, white, ochre, silver, not a slit of any kind in that wonderful nest, only the rustle of those colours waving in the air, impenetrable, lighter than nothingness.

Hervé Joncour did not hear an explosion to blow his life apart. He heard that other sound continue away from him, he felt the rifle-barrel lift from him and heard Hara Kei's softly spoken words:

"Be gone, Frenchman. And don't come back ever again."

———

49

Nothing but silence on the road. The corpse of a little boy on the ground. A man kneeling. Until the last glimmer of daylight.

50

I t took Hervé Joncour eleven days to reach Yokohama. He bribed a Japanese official and procured sixteen boxes of silkworm eggs that came from the south of the island. He wrapped them in silk and sealed them in four round wooden casks. He found a boat to the continent and in the first days of March reached the coast of Russia. He chose the northernmost route, in search of the cold in order to inhibit the life in the eggs and extend the time before they hatched. He made forced marches across four thousand kilometres of Siberia, crossed the Urals, and arrived at Saint Petersburg. He spent a fortune in gold buying ice by the ton and loaded it, together with the eggs, into the hold of a freighter bound for Hamburg. The voyage took six days. He unloaded the four round wooden casks and boarded a southbound train. Eleven hours into the journey, just as they left a town called Eberfeld, the train stopped to take on water. Hervé Joncour looked about him. A summer sun was beating down on the wheat fields, on the world all about. Opposite him sat a Russian merchant; he had taken off his shoes and was fanning himself with the last page of a newspaper written in German. Hervé Joncour gazed at him. He noticed the patches of sweat on the man's shirt and the drops standing out on his forehead and neck. The Russian made some remark and laughed. Hervé Joncour gave him a smile, stood up, collected his bags and stepped off the train. He walked along it to the end wagon, a goods-wagon carrying fish and meat packed in ice. Water was spilling out as from a basin riddled by a thousand bullets. He pulled open the door, climbed into the wagon and took his round wooden casks one by one, carrying them outside and leaving them on the ground beside the track. Then he closed the door again and stopped to wait. When the train was ready to leave they shouted to him to hurry up and get back on board. He replied with a shake of the head and a gesture of farewell. He saw the train move off and disappear in the distance. He waited until he could no longer even hear it. Then he bent over one of his wooden casks, removed the seals and opened it. He did the same with the other three. Slowly, carefully.

Millions of grubs. Dead.

It was 6 May 1865.

———

Hervé joncour entered Lavilledieu nine days later. From a distance his wife Hélène saw the carriage coming up the tree-lined driveway of the property. She told herself that she was not to cry and not to run away.

She went down to the front door, opened it and stopped on the threshold.

When Hervé Joncour reached her, she smiled. He embraced her and quietly said to her:

"Stay with me, please."

That night they stayed up till late, seated beside each other on the lawn in front of their house. Hélène told him about Lavilledieu, about all those months spent waiting, and those ghastly final days.

"You were dead."

She said.

"And in the whole world there was nothing beautiful left."

———

Around the hatcheries of Lavilledieu people looked at the mulberries bursting with foliage and witnessed their own ruin. Baldabiou had found a few consignments of eggs, but the grubs died the moment they saw the light. The raw silk they succeeded in recovering from the few survivors was barely sufficient to give employment to two of the seven mills in the town.

"Have you any ideas?" asked Baldabiou.

"One," replied Hervé Joncour.

The following day he put it about that over the summer months he was going to lay out the park for his villa. He engaged men and women from the town by the dozen. They cleared the hill of timber and somewhat levelled out its profile to give it a gentler slope down to the valley. They used trees and hedges to lay out delicate, transparent mazes. All manner of flowers were used in order to create gardens which opened out like so many unexpected clearings in the heart of little birch-groves. They funnelled water from the river and made it drop from fountain to fountain all the way to the park's western boundary, where it collected in a small lake surrounded by lawns. To the south, amid the lemon and olive trees they built a great aviary out of wood and metal; it looked like an embroidery suspended in mid-air.

It was four months' work. At the end of September the park was ready. At Lavilledieu no one had ever seen anything like it. They said that Hervé Joncour had sunk his entire capital into it. They also said that he had returned from Japan a changed man, maybe a sick one. They said that he had sold the eggs to the Italians and now had a fortune in gold sitting in the Paris banks. They said that were it not for this park they would have starved to death that year. They said he was a swindler. They said he was a saint. Somebody said: There's something about him, like some sort of unhappiness.

———

53

All Hervé Joncour would say about his journey was that the eggs had hatched in a town near Cologne, the place was called Eberfeld.

Four months and thirteen days after his return, Baldabiou sat down opposite him, by the edge of the lake, at the western boundary of the park and said to him:

"At any rate sooner or later you'll have to tell the truth to someone."

He said this slowly with some effort, because he did not believe, he never believed, that the truth served any useful purpose.

Hervé Joncour lifted up his eyes to the park.

It was autumn, with a false light playing all about.

"The first time I saw Hara Kei he was wearing a dark tunic, and sat motionless, cross-legged, in a corner of the room. Lying beside him, her head resting on his lap, was a woman. Her eyes did not have an oriental slant, and her face was the face of a young girl."

Baldabiou listened to him in silence, right to the end, to the train at Eberfeld.

He thought nothing.

He listened.

It pained him to hear Hervé Joncour softly saying, in conclusion:

"I have never even heard her voice."

And a while later:

"It is a strange sort of pain."

Softly.

"To die of yearning for something you'll never experience."

They walked up through the park side by side. The only thing Baldabiou said was:

"What ever is making it so damnably cold?"

That is what he said at a certain point.

———

54

At the beginning of the New Year – 1866 – Japan officially lifted the ban on the export of silkworm eggs.

During the decade that followed, France alone was to import Japanese eggs to the value of ten million francs.

Furthermore, with the opening of the Suez Canal in 1869, Japan could be reached in a voyage of no more than twenty days. A little less than twenty days to return.

Artificial silk was to be patented in 1884 by a Frenchman called Chardonnet.

———

Six months after his return to Lavilledieu Hervé Joncour received through the post a mustard-coloured envelope. On opening it he found seven sheets covered in cramped geometrical writing; black ink; Japanese ideograms. Apart from the name and address on the envelope, there was not a single word written in Western characters. The postage stamps suggested that the letter came from Ostend.

Hervé Joncour fingered it and scrutinised it for a long time. It looked like a catalogue of the footprints of little birds, fanatically meticulous in its compilation. It was surprising to consider that in fact these were signs, that is, the embers of a voice destroyed by fire.

For days on end Hervé Joncour kept the letter with him, folded in two in his pocket. If he changed suits he would transfer it to the new one. He never opened it to look. Every now and then he would finger it, while he was talking with a tenant farmer, or sat on the verandah waiting for it to be dinner-time. One evening he set himself to inspecting it in his study against the light of the lamp. In this transparency, the footprints of the little birds spoke with a muffled voice. What they spoke of was entirely without significance, or else something capable of lifting a life off its hinges: there was no way of knowing, and this was quite satisfactory to Hervé Joncour. He heard Hélène arrive. He set the letter down on the table. She approached him, as she did every night before retiring to her room, and made to kiss him. As she bent over him her nightdress fell open a chink, on her breast. Hervé Joncour noticed that she was wearing nothing underneath, and that her breasts were small and white like those of a young girl.

For four days he continued to lead his life, changing nothing in his measured daily routines. On the morning of the fifth day he put on an elegant grey suit and left for Nîmes. He said he would be home before evening.

At 12 rue Moscat all was as it had been three years earlier. The party was not yet over. The girls were all young and French. The pianist played tunes that sounded Russian; he used the soft pedal. Maybe it was age, maybe some craven sorrow: at the end of each piece he no longer ran his right hand through his hair, . no longer murmured:

"*Voilà.*"

He would stay silent, looking disconcertedly at his hands.

58

Madame Blanche received him without a word. Shiny black hair, oriental features, perfection. Tiny blue flowers on her fingers like so many rings. A long white dress, almost transparent. Bare feet.

Hervé Joncour sat down opposite her. He slipped the letter out of a pocket.

"Do you remember me?"

Madame Blanche gave a barely perceptible nod.

"I need you again."

He passed the letter to her. She had no reason to do so, but she took it and opened it. She looked at the seven sheets, one by one, then raised her eyes to Hervé Joncour.

"I do not care for this language, *monsieur*. I want to forget it, I want to forget that land, and my life there, and everything."

Hervé Joncour sat motionless, his hands grasping the arms of his chair.

"I shall read this letter for you. I shall do it. And I want no money. But I want a promise: never come back to make this request of me."

"You have my word, *madame*."

She looked him in the eye. Then she looked down at the first page of the letter, rice-paper, black ink.

My master and beloved,

she said,

do not be afraid, do not move, keep silent, nobody will see us.

59

*S*tay *like this, I want to look at you, I have looked at you
so much but you were not for me, now you are for me,
don't come close, please, stay as you are, we have a night to
ourselves, and I want to look at you, I've never seen you in
this way, your body for me, your skin, shut your eyes, stroke
yourself, please,*

said Madame Blanche, and Hervé Joncour listened;

*do not open your eyes if you can, and stroke yourself, your
hands are so beautiful, I have dreamed of them so often, now
I want to see them, I like to see them on your skin, like this,
please go on doing it, don't open your eyes, I am here, nobody
can see us and I am close to you, stroke yourself, my master
and beloved, stroke your organ, please, slowly.*

She stopped. Please continue, he said.

*It's beautiful your hand on your organ, don't stop, I love
to look at it and to look at you, my master and beloved, don't
open your eyes, not yet, don't be afraid, I am beside you, do
you feel me? I am here, I can brush you, this is silk, do you
feel it? it's the silk of my dress, don't open your eyes and you'll
have my skin,*

she said; she was reading slowly, with the voice of a
child-woman,

*you'll have my lips, when I touch you for the first time it
will be with my lips, you'll not know where, at a certain point
you will feel the warmth of my lips on you, you can't know
where if you do not open your eyes, don't open them, you'll feel
my lips you know not where, suddenly.*

He listened motionless; from the top pocket of

92

his grey suit a clean white handkerchief protruded.

Perhaps it will be on your eyes, I shall press my mouth to your eyelids and brows, you'll feel the warmth course through your head, and my lips on your eyes, in them, and perhaps it will be on your organ, I shall press my lips there, and I'll part them little by little as I go down,

she said, her head bent over the pages, one hand brushing her neck, slowly,

I'll leave your organ to part my lips, penetrating between my lips, and pressing on my tongue, my saliva will flow down your skin as far as your hand, my kiss and your hand, the one inside the other, on your organ.

He listened, his eyes fixed on a silver picture-frame hanging empty on the wall.

Until in the end I shall kiss you on the heart, because I want you, I shall bite the skin that throbs on your heart, because I want you, and with your heart between my lips you will be mine, truly, with my mouth in your heart you will be mine, forever, if you do not believe me open your eyes, my master and beloved, and look at me, it is I. Who will ever be able to erase this moment that is happening? and this body of mine no longer with any silk, your hands touching it, your eyes looking at it,

she said. She had leaned towards the lamp, the light shone down on the pages and through the transparency of her dress,

your fingers in my cleft, your tongue on my lips, you sliding beneath me, taking me by the hips, lifting me up, letting me slide onto your organ, slowly, who will be able to erase this? you inside me, moving slowly, your hands on my face, your fingers on my mouth, pleasure in your eyes, your voice, you move slowly but to the point of hurting me, my pleasure, my voice.

He listened; at a certain point he turned to look at her, he saw her, he wanted to drop his gaze but could not.

My body on yours, your back lifting me up, your arms that will not let me go, the thrusts inside me, it is sweet violence, I see your eyes probing mine, they want to know how far to go in hurting me, as far as you please, my master and beloved, there is no end, it will not end, don't you see? no one will be able to erase this moment that is happening, you will forever be throwing your head back, crying out, forever I shall shut my eyes, shaking off the tears from my brows, my voice inside yours, your violence in holding me tightly, there is no time left for escaping or strength for resisting, it had to be this moment, and this moment it is, believe me, my master and beloved, this moment shall continue to be, from now on it shall be, till the very end,

she said in a tiny voice, then stopped.

There were no further ideograms on the page she had in her hand: the last page. But when she turned it over to lay it aside she noticed some more lines on the back, all neatly ordered, black ink in the centre of the white page. She raised her eyes to Hervé Joncour. His eyes were fixed on her, and she realised that they were the most beautiful eyes. She lowered hers once more to the page.

We shall not see each other again, my master,

she said.

That which was meant for the two of us, we have done it, as you know, believe me: we have done it for ever. Preserve your life out of my reach. And do not for a moment hesitate,

94

should it be useful for your happiness, to forget this woman who now says to you, without regret, farewell.

For a while she continued to look at the page, then she placed it on top of the others, beside her, on a table made of light-coloured wood. Hervé Joncour did not move. He only turned his head and lowered his eyes. He found himself gazing imperturbably at the pleat of his trousers, perfect if barely perceptible, on his right leg, from thigh to knee.

Madame Blanche stood up, bent over the lamp and put it out. The room remained lit by the little light that reached them through the window from the salon. She approached Hervé Joncour, slipped off her finger a ring of tiny blue flowers and placed it beside him. Then she crossed the room, opened a little painted door concealed in the wall, and disappeared, leaving it slightly ajar behind her.

Hervé Joncour stayed a long time in that strange light, turning a ring of tiny blue flowers round and round in his fingers. From the salon came the notes of a weary piano: they dissolved time, so that you barely recognised it any more.

Eventually he stood up, approached the table made of light-coloured wood, and gathered up the seven sheets of rice-paper. He crossed the room, passed the little half-open door without turning, and left.

60

Hervé Joncour spent the years that followed adhering to the limpid style of living that pertained to a man who stood in need of nothing. He passed his days in a regime of measured emotions. At Lavilledieu he came once more to be admired as people seemed to recognise in him a *precise* method of belonging in the world. They said he had been this way even as a young man, before Japan.

He adopted the habit of making a little journey each year with his wife Hélène. They saw Naples, Rome, Madrid, Munich, London. One year they went as far afield as Prague, where everything seemed to be: theatre. They travelled unmindful of dates, of programmes. They found astonishment in everything: secretly even in their happiness. When they felt the call of silence, they would return to Lavilledieu.

Had he been asked, Hervé Joncour would have replied that this was how they were going to go on living, forever. He had about him the unassailable tranquillity of men who feel at ease with themselves. Occasionally, on windy days, he would cross the park as far as the lake and stop on the shore for hours to watch the ripples on the surface of the water, as they made unpredictable patterns that glinted at random, in every direction. The wind was one and one alone: but it seemed as though a thousand were blowing upon that mirror-surface. From every direction. A spectacle. Light and unsearchable.

Occasionally, on windy days Hervé Joncour would go down to the lake and spend hours in contemplation of it because he seemed to descry, sketched out on the water, the inexplicable sight of his life as it had been, in all its lightness.

———

61

On 16 June 1871, in the back of the Café Verdun, shortly before noon, the handicapped player chalked up a cannon off four cushions for no reason, and evened the score. Baldabiou leaned over the table in disbelief, one hand behind his back, the other grasping his cue.

"Fancy that!"

He straightened up, put away his cue and went out without saying goodbye. Three days later he left. He made a gift of his two mills to Hervé Joncour.

"I want nothing more to do with silk, Baldabiou."

"Sell them, you ass."

Nobody succeeded in extracting from him where the devil he intended to go. And to do what once he got there. He simply dropped something about Saint Agnes that nobody really grasped.

On the morning of his departure Hervé Joncour, together with Hélène, accompanied him as far as the railway station at Avignon. All he had with him was one suitcase, and this in itself was not a little indecipherable. When he saw the train waiting at the platform he set the case down.

"I once knew a man who built a railway all for himself."

He said.

"And d'you know what? He built it straight as an arrow, hundreds of kilometres without a single curve.

There was a reason, but I can't recall what it was. Reasons get forgotten. Anyway – goodbye."

He was not really cut out for serious discussions. And a goodbye is a serious matter.

They saw him leave, him and his suitcase, forever.

Then Hélène did an odd thing. She pulled free of Hervé Joncour and ran after him until she caught him up, and she embraced him tightly, and as she embraced him she burst into tears.

Hélène never cried.

Hervé Joncour sold the two mills for a song to Michel Lariot, a stout fellow who had been playing dominoes with Baldabiou every Saturday evening for twenty years, and always lost, with indefectible consistency. He had three girls. The two eldest were called Florence and Sylvie. But the third: Agnes.

———

62

Three years later, in the winter of 1874, Hélène fell ill with a cerebral fever that no physician was able to diagnose nor to cure. She died at the beginning of March, a day when it rained.

The whole of Lavilledieu turned out to accompany her in silence up the avenue of the cemetery: she had been a good-humoured woman and had not caused grief to anyone.

On her tomb Hervé Joncour had a single word carved.

"*Hélas.*"

He thanked everyone, said time and again that he had need of nothing, and returned home. Never had it seemed to him so big; and never had his fate seemed to him so illogical.

Inasmuch as despair was an excess that had no part in him, he concentrated on what was left of his life and began once more to give it his attention, with the unshakeable tenacity of a gardener back at work the morning after the storm.

63

Two months and eleven days after Hélène's death Hervé Joncour happened to visit the cemetery and there he found, beside the roses which every week he laid upon his wife's grave, a little garland of tiny blue flowers. He bent over to look at them and remained for ages in that posture; from a distance it could not have failed to appear to the casual observer as totally bizarre if not actually ridiculous. On his return home he did not go out to work in the park, as was his custom, but stayed in his study, thinking. He did nothing else, for days. Thinking.

64

At 12 rue Moscat he found a tailor's shop. He was told that Madame Blanche had not lived there for years. He succeeded in discovering that she had moved to Paris, where she had become the mistress of a very important person, maybe a politician.

Hervé Joncour went to Paris.

It took him six days to find out where she lived. He sent her a note asking for an appointment. She answered to say she was expecting him at four o'clock the next day. Punctually he climbed the stairs to the second floor of an elegant mansion on the boulevard des Capucines. A maid opened the door to him. She brought him into the drawing-room and asked him to take a seat. Madame Blanche arrived in a very elegant, very French costume. Her hair fell to her shoulders as Paris fashion dictated. On her fingers she was not wearing any ring of blue flowers. She sat down opposite Hervé Joncour, without a word. And waited.

He looked her in the eye. But the way a child might have done.

"It was you who wrote that letter, wasn't it?"

He said.

"Hélène asked you to write it and you did so."

Madame Blanche sat motionless; she did not lower her eyes, did not betray the smallest surprise.

Then what she said was:

"It was not I who wrote it."

Silence.

"It was Hélène who wrote that letter."

Silence.

"When she came to me she had already written it. She asked me to copy it out, in Japanese. And I did so. That is the truth."

In that instant Hervé Joncour understood that he was to continue hearing those words for the rest of his life. He stood up, but remained standing, as if he had suddenly forgotten where he was bound for. The voice of Madame Blanche reached him as from a distance.

"She even wanted to read it to me, that letter. She had the most beautiful voice. And she read those words with an emotion that I've never been able to forget. It was as if they really were her own words."

Hervé Joncour was crossing the room, very slowly.

"You know, *monsieur*, I believe that she would have wanted, more than anything in the world, to have been *that woman*. You can't understand. But I heard her read that letter. I know."

Hervé Joncour had reached the door. He rested his hand on the doorhandle. Without turning he slowly said:

"Farewell, *madame*."

They never saw each other again.

———

65

Hervé Joncour lived for a further twenty-three years, most of them marked by serenity and good health. He never again left Lavilledieu, nor even quit his house. He managed his estate wisely, and this preserved him from the need ever to have to undertake any work other than the upkeep of his own park. In time he began to allow himself a pleasure that hitherto he had always denied himself: he would talk of his travels to those who came to call on him. As they listened to him, the folk of Lavilledieu discovered the world, and the children learned what it was to marvel. He would tell his tales slowly, seeing in the air things that the others did not see.

On Sundays he would go into town for High Mass. Once a year he would make the round of the mills, to touch the newly-born silk. When loneliness mastered him he would go up to the cemetery and talk to Hélène. The rest of his time was taken up with a liturgy of habits that succeeded in warding off sadness. Occasionally, on windy days, he would go down to the lake and spend hours in contemplation of it because he seemed to descry, sketched out on the water, the inexplicable sight of his life as it had been, in all its lightness.